أُغُسْطَس وبسمتُهُ

Augustus and his Smile

Text and Illustrations copyright © Catherine Rayner 2006
Catherine Raynor has asserted her right to be identified as the author and
illustrator of this work under the Copyright, Designs and Patents Act, 1988
Dual language copyright © Mantra Lingua 2008
Printed Paola, Malta MP210217PB03171693

Mantra Lingua
303 Ballards Lane, London N12 8NP
www.mantralingua.com

First published in UK
This edition published 2017
by Little Tiger Press 2006

Audio copyright ©
Mantra Lingua 2008

Thank you, Mum, Brian and Colin - C R

أغُـــــطُـــس وبَـــسمَـــتَـــهُ

Augustus and his Smile

Catherine Rayner

Arabic translation by
Wafa' Tarnowska

MANTRA
LINGUA

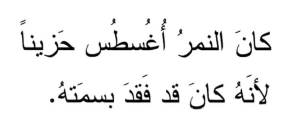

كانَ النمرُ أُغُسطُس حَزيناً
لأنَهُ كانَ قد فَقدَ بسمَتهُ.

Augustus the tiger was sad.
He had lost his smile.

فمدَّدَ جسـدَه مَدّةَ النمرِ العظيمةِ ثُمَ ذَهبَ يَبحَثُ عليها.

So he did a HUGE tigery stretch and set off to find it.

في البدىء إنسلَّ تحتَ كُتلةِ
شُجيراتٍ فوجَدَ خنُفُساءَ
صَغيرةٍ تَلمَع ،
لكِنَهُ لم يجِد بسمتَه.

First he crept under a cluster
of bushes. He found a small,
shiny beetle, but he couldn't
see his smile.

Then he climbed to the tops of the tallest trees.
He found birds that chirped and called,
but he couldn't find his smile.

ثُمَ تسلّقَ أعلى أعالي الأشجارِ.
فوجَدَ عصافيراً تُزقزِقُ وتُنادي ،
لكنَهُ لم يجِد بسمَتهُ.

فتّش أغُسطُس بعيداً بعيداً.

تسلّقَ أعلى أعالي الجِبالِ حَيثُ الغيومُ

الثّلجيةِ تدورُ وتلتَفُ راسِمةً أشكالاً في

الهواءِ المجلّدِ المصقِعِ.

Further and further Augustus searched.
He scaled the crests of the highest mountains where the
snow clouds swirled, making frost patterns in the freezing air.

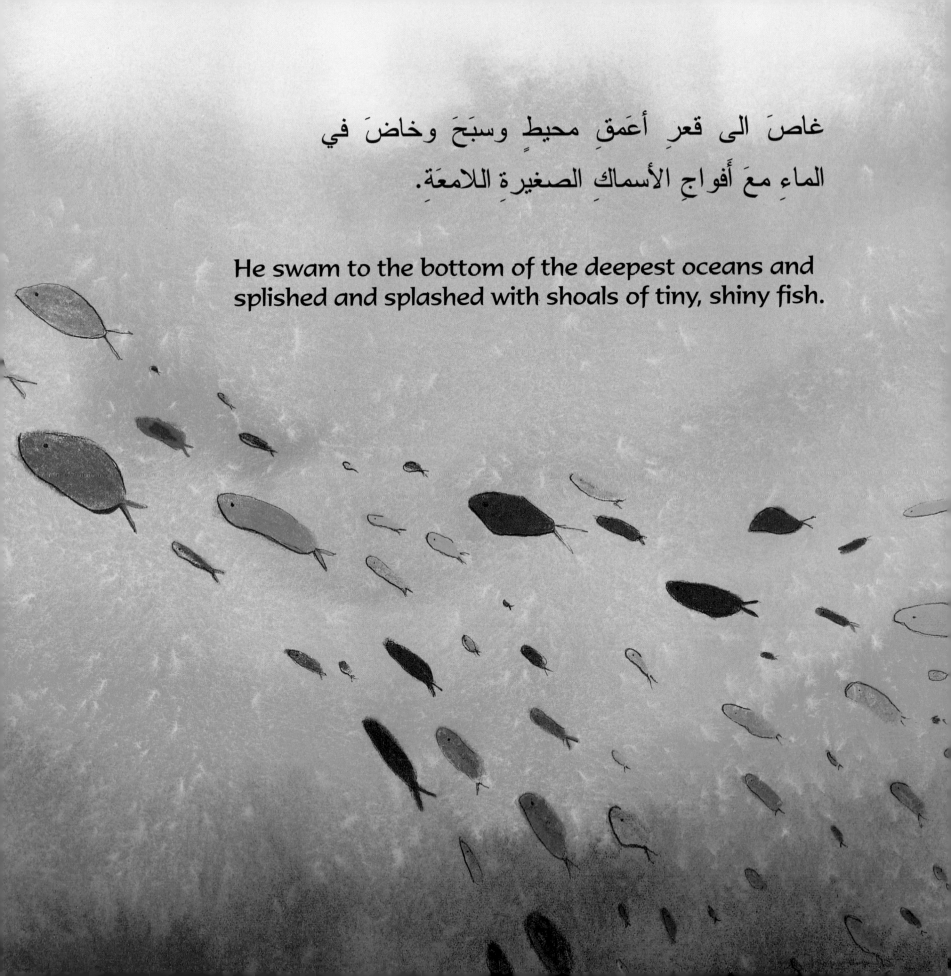

غاصَ الى قعرِ أَعَمقِ محيطٍ وسبَحَ وخاضَ في الماءِ معَ أَفواجِ الأسماكِ الصغيرةِ اللامعَةِ.

He swam to the bottom of the deepest oceans and splished and splashed with shoals of tiny, shiny fish.

تبخترَ وتباهى ماشياً في أوسَعِ صحراءٍ محّوِلاً
خيالهُ إلى أشكالٍ في الشمسِ. ثم مشى أبعَد
وأبعَد بين الرمال المتحركَةِ
إلى أن ...

He pranced and paraded through
the largest desert, making
shadow shapes in the sun.
Augustus padded further
and further
through shifting sand
until...

... pitter patter

pitter patter

drip

drop

plop!

... طُق

طق

طق

طق

نقطة

نقطة

قطرة

قطرة!

رقص أغُسطُس
وتسابَق
وحبّاتُ المطرِ تقعُ
وتطير.

Augustus danced
and raced
as raindrops bounced
and flew.

خاضَ في حُفَرِ ماءٍ أكبَرَ وأعمق. أسرَعَ نحو

حفرةٍ مائيةٍ كبيرةٍ زرقاءَ وفضيّةٍ فرأى ...

He splashed through puddles, bigger and deeper.
He raced towards a huge silver-blue puddle
and saw ...

... هنا تحتَ أَنفِ

... أنفِــهِ!

... there under his nose
... his smile!

عندَها، أدركَ أغُسطُس أنّ بسمتَهُ تكونُ موجودةً عندَما يكونُ سعيداً.

ما علَيهِ إلا أن يسبَحَ معَ الأسماك أو يرقُصَ في حُفَرِ الماءِ، أو يتسلّقَ الجبَالِ

أو ينظُرَ الى العالَم – لأنّ السعادةَ كانَت حَولَهُ في كَلّ مكانٍ.

كان أغسطُس سعيداً جداً فوثَبَ ونطَّ ...

And Augustus realised that his smile would be there, whenever he was happy.

He only had to swim with the fish or dance in the puddles, or climb the mountains and look at the world – for happiness was everywhere around him.

Augustus was so pleased that
he hopped
and skipped ...

... وقفزَ مبتعِداً وهو يبتسَم.

... and jumped away,
smiling.

Amazing tiger facts

Augustus is a Siberian tiger.

Siberian tigers are the biggest cats in the world! They live in Southern Russia and Northern China where the winters are very cold.

Most tigers are orange with black stripes. The stripes make them hard to see when they walk through tall weeds and grasses.

Tigers are good swimmers and like to cool down by sitting in waterholes.

Each tiger's stripes are different to those of other tigers – like a human finger print.

Tigers are in danger …

Tigers are only hunted by one animal … HUMANS!And humans are ruining the land on which tigers live.

There are more tigers living in zoos and nature reserves than in the wild. There are only about 6000 tigers left in the wild.

Help save the tiger!

World Wildlife Fund (WWF)
Panda House
Weyside Park
Godalming
Surrey GU7 1XR
Tel: 01483 426 444
www.wwf.org.uk

David Shepherd Wildlife
Foundation
61 Smithbrook Kilns
Cranleigh
Surrey GU76 8JJ
Tel: 01483 727 323/267 924
www.davidshepherd.org